Baby's Christmas

W9-COV-695

By Esther Wilkin
Revised by Diane Muldrow

Illustrated by Barbara Lanza
In homage to Eloise Wilkin – BL

GOLDEN BOOKS ™ **A GOLDEN BOOK • NEW YORK**

Golden Books Publishing Company, Inc., New York, New York 10106

It's Baby's first Christmas!
Let's go and see
What Santa has left for you
Under the tree.

Baby loves the Christmas tree
With candy canes and
twinkling lights,

Tiny angels of silver and gold,
And colored balls so shiny
and bright!

Baby, look what Santa brought!
A string of beads, bright white and blue,
A rattle and a stack of blocks,
And a doll that looks like you.

Santa left a teddy bear,

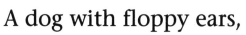
A dog with floppy ears,

A child's drum to beat upon,

A little car that steers.

Santa left a rubber ball
To roll along the floor,

A picture book,
A kitty cat,
And much, much more—

A rocking horse,

A bouncy swing,

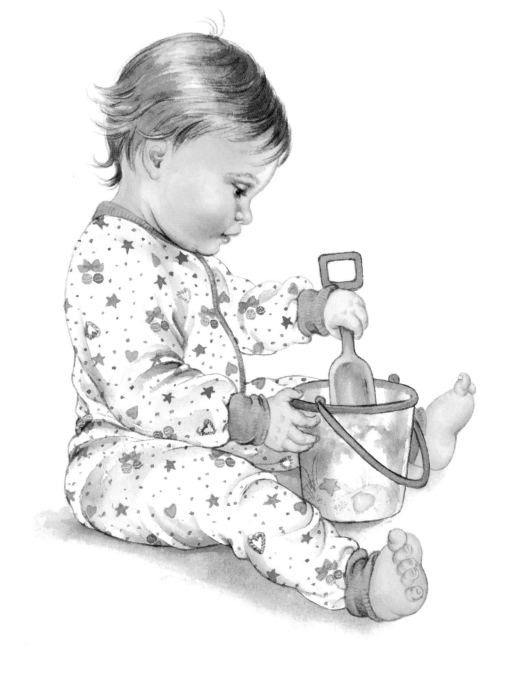

A shovel and a pail,

A rubber duck,
A wooden boat
For a little one to sail.

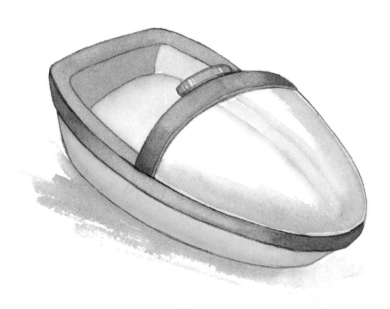

Santa left a Noah's ark,

A fire truck,

A train—

A little wagon you can pull
To there and back again.

Baby, Santa has been good to you.
You've played and played this whole
 day through.
You've had a happy Christmas Day—
Now it's time to put your toys away.

You look so sleepy, Baby!
Let's turn out the light.
Sleep tight, our dear little one.
Merry Christmas, and good night.